PICK YOUR POISON

IN LOVING MEMORY OF MARSHA SMITH AND DEMICO KING.

To my children: you may face a thousand losses on your journey, but each one will build the strength, wisdom, and skill you need to make your dreams come true. Every loss prepares you to win ten times greater than you ever imagined.

Love, Mom

Table of Contents

1. LOVE IS PAIN
2. DAILY DOSES
3. COST OF BETRAYAL
4. THE REKON OF ROLUNISIS
5. THE TRUTH SHE BURIED
6. THE ONE SHE LET HAPPEN
7. THE FIRE SHE LIT AND WALKED AWAY FROM
8. THE MOMENT THEY COULD HAVE STOPPED IT
9. SHADOWS OF CHAIN

CHAPTER 1- Love is Pain

My mother's scream split the warehouse just as my finger tightened around the trigger of my father's .45.

The gunshot echoed off cold concrete and rusted steel. Vaughn's body jerked, then collapsed hard against the warehouse floor, the sound of bone against cement louder than the ringing in my ears.

For a second, the world froze.

Then my mother ran.

She dropped to her knees beside him, pulling his lifeless body into her arms like she could still save him. Blood soaked into her clothes, dark and spreading, staining the floor the way this moment would stain me forever.

"This is your father," she sobbed. "I was going to tell you... I swear I was. When I got back from Atlanta—"

Her words blurred together as the weight of what I'd done crushed down on my chest.

I know you're probably wondering how we got here.

So let me take you back—

Back to where the streets first taught me that blood always comes due.

———————

The Beginning

"Azaliyah. Jonsai."

My father's voice was barely louder than a whisper, but it carried the kind of urgency that snapped you awake instantly.

"Get up. Come to my man cave. Now. I need to tell you girls something important."

Important usually meant drills.

Guns. Escape routes. What to do if men kicked the door in while we slept.

My father wasn't just anyone. He was the biggest drug dealer in New York City. Brooklyn. Harlem. The Bronx. Manhattan. Queens. Every borough answered to him in one way or another.

So when Jonsai—my older sister—and I slipped on our house shoes and followed him down the hallway, we already knew tonight wasn't going to be normal.

He looked different. Tired. Edges frayed. The kind of tired that comes when death has already whispered your name.

"I'm going away for a while," he said quietly. "Word on the street is Vaughn's sending someone after me tomorrow."

My stomach dropped.

"I love you girls more than anything," he continued. "And whatever happens... remember what I taught you."

That was the last time I saw him alive.

The next morning, Jonsai and I got dressed for school like everything was normal. Like our world hadn't cracked open overnight. Mom usually drove us when she was home—but neither of our parents were there.

So we caught the bus.

And as we walked toward the corner, I couldn't shake the feeling that the streets were watching us... waiting for their turn.

As we walked toward the bus stop, a BMW crept up beside us, tires whispering against the pavement. The window slid down slow.

Too slow.

"What's good?!" Jonsai called out, already squared up. She stayed ready. Daddy made sure of that. We stayed strapped, and we were taught one thing—shoot to kill.

Vaughn leaned out the window, smiling like the devil knew your secrets.

"Relax," he said. "I'm just riding by to speak to Azaliyah."
His eyes dragged over me. "What's up, mama? I can't wait till you turn eighteen."
He laughed. "Hell... seventeen legal too."

My skin crawled.

He blew me a kiss, rolled the window back up, and sped off in his brand-new BMW like he hadn't just poisoned the air around us.

"One day I'm gonna kill him," Jonsai snapped. "Who the fuck hits on a thirteen-year-old?"

"And knowing how he talking to us," I said quietly, my chest tight, "and he done put a hit out on Daddy?"

Jonsai looked at me.
I looked back.

That look said everything.
Exactly. B. What the fuck.

We got on the bus, but I barely remember the ride.

The whole day I was quiet.

You ever get that feeling like something bad is hunting you? Like your stomach twists, your heart races, and your hands will not stop shaking.

That is how I felt all day.

RING! RING!

The final bell screamed through the school.

When Jonsai and I stepped outside, Daddy was waiting for us. The relief hit so hard I almost cried. We ran straight into his arms.

"Come on," he said, kissing our heads. "Let me take my girls to get something to eat."

As we drove, we saw my uncle and cousins in the street—arguing, shoving, chaos spilling everywhere. Daddy pulled over at once.

He hated family drama.

"WE ALL WE GOT!" he shouted.
"Fight for what?! Let's get a bag together! Let's make history, baby!"

He stepped out to break it up.

Then—

POW! POW!

Gunshots tore through the air.

Everything froze.

People screamed.
"HEDRICK!"
"HEDRIIICK!"

My heart stopped.

Jonsai jumped out the car, screaming, running toward Daddy.

I didn't think.

I grabbed Daddy's .380 and jumped out.

A man dressed all in black was pointing down the street, already running.
The world narrowed to him.

I raised the gun.

I fired.
Again.
Again.

I did not stop until the trigger clicked empty.

The man dropped to his knees.

Uncle Ty snatched the gun from my hands, wrapped it up fast, and tucked it into his waistband like it was just another street secret.

I ran to my father and held him until the ambulance came.

Blood soaked through my clothes. Through my hands. I kept telling him to stay with me, like my voice alone could pull him back. When the paramedics finally took him, they wouldn't let Jonsai or me ride along.

So, we called our mother.

A few days later, we buried my father.

Closed casket.

I never understood why back then. I told myself it was because I was young—too young to see what bullets really do to a body. Too young to understand how violent death rearranges a man.

All I knew was this:
My father was gone.

He left us five point six million dollars and a letter. In it, he told us how much he loved us. How proud he was. And that if anything ever happened to him, he'd made sure we'd never need for anything—not money, not protection, not answers.

But money doesn't fill graves.

A year passed.

I was sitting in my eighth-grade classroom when a boy walked in late. The room shifted immediately.

"Attention, class," the teacher said. "This is Jacques. He's our new student. Please show him the ropes."

Girls whispered. Heads turned. Somebody giggled.

He was cute. Everyone noticed.

But he didn't sit with them.

He sat next to me.

The room went quiet.

Everyone knew who my father was. Everyone knew how he died. Nobody ever tried me—or Jonsai. We were city royalty wrapped in tragedy.

Jacques and I started as friends. Real friends. The kind that sits in silence and don't need to fill it. Over time, that friendship deepened into something people mistook for marriage.

We never rushed it. Never needed labels.

We double-dated with Jonsai and Devin. They'd been talking since second grade—soulmates before they even knew what love was.

Years flew by.

And then—

The Plot

My eighteenth birthday arrived, and I sat alone in my room, staring at the ceiling, choking on the same ache that visited me every year.

My father should've been here.

That's when the thought came.

Cold. Clear. Complete.

I should set this nigga up.

Not rushed. Not sloppy.

I'd earn his trust. Make him comfortable. Let his guards lower theirs. Let him believe I was curious… interested… harmless.

Then I'd end him.

A life for a life.

I wiped my face, stood up, and went to my closet.

All black. Fitted dress.
Messy bun.
Fendi shades—black with gold trim.
Black furry slides with the gold chain.

If I was going to do this, I was going to do it right.

Downstairs, the kitchen buzzed with birthday energy.

"How it feel to finally be eighteen ?" Jonsai asked, smiling.

"My baby is beautiful," my mom said. "Happy birthday again. Come outside—I've got a surprise."

In the driveway sat a 2015 Porsche 918 Spyder.

I screamed and snatched the keys.

Two months ago, I'd mentioned it casually. Didn't think she remembered. Didn't think she'd actually do it.

I told her I was taking it for a spin.

Once I pulled out the driveway, the plan started moving.

I drove to the store I knew Vaughn would be at. Walked in like I was buying something small.

Right on cue, he followed.

He grabbed my arm.

"Azaliyah," he said, voice slick. "You pulled up looking like a whole soul food meal. When you gone let me show you what real is?"

I turned and looked him dead in his face.

"What can you give me," I asked, "that I don't already have?"

He smiled like he'd already won.

"Put your number in my phone. I'll text you an address. Meet me there. Dress sexy."

I put my number in his phone.

Then I drove home.

I didn't tell Jonsai. She would've shut it down immediately. This was something I had to do alone.

And with everything my father taught me—

I knew I could pull it off.

I got back to the house and tried to enjoy my birthday party. The music, the laughter, the cake—it all felt fake. Like I was playing a role.

Around 9:30 p.m., Vaughn texted me an address.

I told my mom I was going out to eat with a friend. Jonsai helped me with my makeup, unaware of the war I was about to walk into. I went to my closet and pulled out the sexiest dress and heels I owned.

If I was going to do this, I was going to look unforgettable.

As soon as I pulled up to the address, my phone buzzed again.

Jacques.

Come see me. I got a surprise for you.

We'd made our relationship official a few months back, so I knew he was probably planning something special. My chest tightened. I had never lied to him—not once.

But revenge was louder than guilt.

I texted him back that I was at my cousin's house visiting my grandmother for my birthday… then turned my phone off.

The gate buzzed open.

I drove down a long private path that led to a massive mansion. All I could think was how this man was living lavish while my father was in the ground.

I parked, stepped out, and walked toward the door.

Before I could knock, it opened.

Soft music floated through the air. Vaughn stood there smiling, maids and a chef behind him like props in a movie.

"Come in," he said. "Make yourself at home. They're here to make sure you're comfortable."

I handed my jacket and purse to the maid and followed him inside.

The table was covered in food and desserts I couldn't pronounce. He poured champagne, pulled my chair out, and waited until I sat.

"Are you comfortable?" he asked. "Can I get you anything?"

"I'm good," I said calmly. "What's all this for?"

He smiled slow.

"For you. I've wanted you for years. You were too young back then… but now?"

He leaned closer. "Now you grown."

My stomach turned, but my face didn't show it.

"I want to taste you," he said.

I let him believe that hunger was mutual.

He closed the distance between us, touching me like he already owned me. I dissociated—just enough. I focused on my breathing. On my father's voice. On the plan.

When he touched me, I let my body react even while my mind stayed somewhere else. Every sound, every movement, I memorized.

This wasn't love.

This was infiltration.

When it was over, when I lay there staring at the ceiling, I felt something inside me harden—not break.

I wasn't his.

He was already dead.

He just didn't know it yet.

But I stuck to the plan.

Take everything he had...
then take his life.

After that night, my world became a balancing act I could never drop. School. Jacques. Vaughn. Every day felt like walking a tightrope over concrete.

Vaughn flew me to his house in Dallas every other weekend. Jacques's people lived in Dallas too, but I'd never met them. That was the blessing. The cover.

I kept it up for almost a year.

Nobody knew about me and Vaughn. Not my sister. Not my mother. Not Jacques.

Then one day, Vaughn looked at me differently.

Like he was testing the weight of my loyalty.

"I need you to prove you really down for me," he said. "Set Jacques up."

My heart didn't skip. It hardened.

"I'll do it," I told him. "But you don't kill him."

He studied me for a long moment, then nodded.

We planned everything carefully.

And waited.

The Set Up

I came home from school and dropped my backpack on the floor, collapsing onto the couch like my body had finally run out of lies.

Jonsai stared at me.
"What's wrong with you? You look all soft and in love." She laughed. "And Mom said she's going out of town for two weeks, so I'm in charge. No boys allowed in the house."

We both cracked up, knowing damn well Devin and Jacques would be everywhere.

"Me and Jacques had our first real kiss today," I said, kicking my shoes off. "It made me feel… light. Like my chest opened up."

Jonsai squinted at me.
"Don't tell me you thinking about losing your v-card on my watch. Mom will kill both of us."

She got serious then.

"All jokes aside, I want you happy. Don't rush nothing. If he loves you, he'll wait. You eighteen. You beautiful. College right around the corner."

She had no idea.

No idea what I'd already given up.
No idea what I was planning to take back.

"I'm not ready for sex anyway," I said smoothly.

Right then, my phone rang.

"AZALIYAH!" Keisha screamed through the speaker. "Party tonight at the Omni. You and JoJo better pull up!"

I smiled into the lie.
"Say less. I'm finna tell JoJo now."

I hung up.

And just like that, the pieces started sliding into place.

Jonsai and I got dressed and headed out in her car.

The moment we walked into the Omni, Keisha spotted us and shouted like royalty had arrived. The DJ ran it back, bottles popped, and the party jumped all the way off.

About an hour in, Keisha leaned close to me.
"Girl... there go your man."

I turned.

Jacques had just walked in.

I didn't think — I ran. Jumped into his arms like the night needed to know we were solid.

"Damn," he laughed, holding me tight. "I was hoping I'd see you. You just made my whole night, baby girl. You hungry? Thirsty? Whatever you want, I got you."

"I'm good," I said, smiling. "Let's just have fun tonight. No worries."
I stepped back just enough to tease him. "And look — your favorite color."

He bit his lip, hand on his chin.
"Yeah... you look real nice. Matter fact, you look good enough to eat."
Then, softer: "I booked a room here tonight. I want you to stay with me."

I agreed.

Our song came on, and we met in the middle of the dance floor. The music wrapped around us, the lights flashing, bodies moving. For a moment, the world narrowed to rhythm and breath.

Keisha yelled over the music to Jonsai, "I love watching Liyah dance — she got these boys going crazy! Jacques can dance too. I know they chemistry crazy!"

Jonsai rolled her eyes.
"Just 'cause they can dance don't mean they doing anything. My little sister ain't rushing nothing."

Then she laughed. "But me? Devin finna get all this attention tonight. Tequila talking."

Keisha screamed laughing. "I love you, JoJo! Midnight hit — everybody either leaving or heading upstairs. I'm getting gone!"

I found Jonsai before we left and told her I was staying the night.

She grabbed my arm.
"Remember what I said earlier. Only when you ready. I mean that."

I nodded, hugged her, and walked out with Jacques.

We stopped by my place to grab clothes, then headed back.

In the elevator, I leaned in and kissed him. He squeezed my hand as the doors opened.

The room took my breath away.

Rose petals everywhere. A Jacuzzi filled with fruit and milk bath, candles glowing low. On the bed sat two oversized gift bags, a teddy bear between them, my name written across the card.

"You did all this… for me?" I whispered. "Why? This is beautiful."

He smiled.
"You deserve it. Start by getting in the tub. Relax."

He helped me with my heels, gentle, patient.
"I ordered dinner," he said. "It'll be here soon. Just tell me what you need."

I sank into the warm water, music humming through the room, the night finally quiet. Jacques sat back, giving me space, controller in hand, like he wasn't trying to own the moment — just share it.

Thirty minutes later, a knock.

Jacques answered the door as the server rolled in dinner, setting the table with care.

"Anything else tonight, sir?" the waiter asked.

"That's perfect," Jacques said, handing him a generous tip.

When the door closed, I watched the steam rise from the plates… and felt the weight of the lie I was living settle deeper into my chest.

Because somewhere between the rose petals and the candles, I realized something terrifying:

This was the life I was pretending to want.
And the other one — the one soaked in blood and secrets — was already pulling me back.

Then—

BOOM.

The door exploded open.

POW! POW!

Gunfire ripped through the room.

Jacques dropped hard, crashing to the floor as blood splashed across white tile.

"GRAB THAT BITCH!" a voice barked.
"The jet'll be here in fifteen!"

Men dressed in all black stormed in. One of them yanked me by the arm as I screamed, my throat tearing apart.

Another dragged Jacques upright and slammed him against the tub. He was barely conscious, bleeding from his arm and side. Someone shoved a phone into his shaking hand.

"Man—hello?!" Jacques grunted. "Who is this?!"

The voice on the other end was calm. Cold.

"Vaughn," he said. "If you wanna see your girl again, I better have one million in forty-eight hours. Miss that deadline, and I'm sending her head to your mama's house."

The line went dead.

I was dragged out kicking and screaming, my nails clawing at the floor.

"AZALIYAH!" Jacques screamed after me. "I'M COMING FOR YOU, BABY!"

The door slammed.

Jacques crawled across the floor, blood slick beneath him. He grabbed his phone and a crumpled piece of paper one of the men had tossed onto the bed.

He dialed with trembling hands.

"MAN!" he yelled when the call connected. "THIS NIGGA NAMED VAUGHN JUST SNATCHED MY GIRL! I'M SHOT—ARM AND SIDE!"

The voice on the other end snapped sharp.

"VAUGHN?!"
"I'm on my way. Stay alive, Jacques."

The phone slipped from his hand as his body gave out.

"Jacques at the Omni!" the man barked into another call. "He's been shot and ain't saying shit. Get up there now!"

Then, louder—to everyone in the room—
"EVERYBODY ELSE, MEET ME AT THE OFFICE IN THIRTY. I WANT THE WHOLE FAMILY THERE!"

They got Jacques to the hospital just in time.

"He lost a lot of blood," Kadien said as he walked into the room. "But he's stable. Doctors say he's gonna be okay."

"Did he tell you who took his girl?" Hedrick asked.

Kadien started to answer—then stopped. His eyes flicked toward the door.

The doctor walked in.

"He's going to be fine," the doctor said. "We removed both bullets. With rest, he should make a full recovery."

"Thank you," Hedrick said calmly, shaking his hand. "We'll take it from here."

"Alright," Kadien said once they were alone. "Let's roll."

They helped me into a wheelchair and pushed me out.

Out of the hospital.
Into the night.
Straight toward the storm.

THE OFFICE

The Office was an abandoned building Hedrick had bought years ago. No signs. No cameras. No neighbors asking questions.

Business happened there.

Blood business.

When we pulled up, everyone was already inside.

Hedrick sat at the round table and waited until the room went silent.

Whatever was about to be said next—

was going to change everything.

The round table meant one thing.

Shit was about to get serious.

Hedrick leaned forward, hands flat on the wood.
"Alright. Vaughn's father was an enemy of my father back in the day. His crew killed my pops and took over his business. When I came of age, me and Vaughn started clashing."

The room stayed quiet.

"I shot his crew. They shot at mine. Four years ago, me and my people robbed him for ten million. He sent someone to kill me after that."

Jacques slammed his hands on the table.
"What the fuck that got to do with my girl?! He asking me for a million. How he even know about us?"

Kadien shook his head slowly.
"Something ain't right."

Hedrick looked at Jacques.
"Where he say to meet?"

Jacques pulled the paper from his pocket and slid it across the table.

Hedrick read it once. Then again.

"KAD," he said. "Call the jet. We need to be in Dallas immediately."
Then to everyone else:
"Everybody else—trap up."

Azaliyah Arrives in Dallas

"Bae, you could've at least gave me a heads up," I said lightly as I walked into Vaughn's Dallas house. "But did you get my food?"

I had to play it cool.

But the whole flight my chest felt tight. I wanted to call Jacques so bad. Tell him everything. Explain why I disappeared.

I hoped he wouldn't hate me for what I was doing.

"Yes, baby," Vaughn said, irritation laced through his voice. "You had to be surprised so it would look real. That nigga better come up with that money."

"Oh, he will," I said, forcing a laugh. "He crazy about me."

I started toward the shower, my mind racing.

"Did you tell your sister about the pregnancy?" Vaughn asked. "I thought I wasn't gone see you again, so I had to act fast."

My stomach dropped.

I didn't answer right away.

"There's too much going on," I finally said. "I'll tell her when all this is over."

"You need to," Vaughn snapped. "You not raising my baby in New York."

I showered, then sat alone on the balcony, staring out at the city lights.

Security everywhere.
Eyes always watching.

And less than twenty-four hours left before the money drop.

Fuck.

I knew I had to move soon—or walk away entirely.

"The food is here, Ms. Azaliyah," the house cleaner said softly. "Vaughn asked if you want it brought up or if you'd like to sit at the table."

"I'll come down," I said, standing.

As I followed her, I made my decision.

I'd make my move at the meet.

Let Vaughn see who really had control.

New York Comes to Dallas

"Keisha," Jonsai said urgently, phone pressed to her ear. "You heard from Liyah?"

"No," Keisha replied. "But Jacques got shot at the Omni last night. Somebody broke into the room. It's all over Facebook."

Jonsai froze.

"God… please let my sister be okay."
Then, sharper: "Find out everything you can. Who took her. What happened. If Mom finds out before we do, she'll kill me."

Keisha started making calls.

Within the hour, the girls gathered at Jonsai's house.

"JoJo," Keisha said, breathless. "I confirmed it. Vaughn has Liyah. He demanding one million from Jacques. Jacques and his crew left for Dallas less than two hours ago—private jet."

Jonsai's face went cold.

"Vaughn?" she whispered.
Then rage hit.
"That's the nigga who had my daddy killed."

Her hands balled into fists.

"I'm going to kill that bitch."

Call Devin," Jonsai said urgently. "We got people in Dallas. Somebody knows something. And if we leave without telling him, he'll kill us both."

Courtney—Devin's twin—nodded.
"She right."

Devin met us at the airport ten minutes later.

We boarded the jet in silence.

Midair, Devin called his uncle.

"Unc," he said. "We on our way to Dallas. A nigga named Vaughn took my girl little sister."

There was a pause.

"…Vaughn?" his uncle said slowly. "The drug lord?"

"Yes."

"How she look?"

"She light-skinned. About five-one. Long hair—"

"Stop," his uncle cut in. "Her name wouldn't happen to be Azaliyah… would it?"

My stomach dropped.

"That's her," I snapped, grabbing the phone. "What you mean his girl?"

"They been together," he said. "Everybody down here know that. Word is… she pregnant too."

The jet felt like it tilted.

"She pregnant?" I screamed. "You saying my sister is Vaughn's girl?!"

Something was terribly wrong.

"Big meeting in about five hours," his uncle continued. "How long till y'all touch down?"

"Two hours," Devin said, taking the phone back.

When the call ended, I broke.

"This don't make sense!" I cried.

Devin pulled me into his chest.
"We gonna get answers. I promise you."

Dallas

As we landed, Keisha pointed toward the parking lot.

"That's Jacques."

He climbed into an all-black SUV.

"Track his phone," Alexus said. "We need his moves."

Keisha smirked.
"Already on it."

Devin's uncle picked us up and took us straight to his house.

"Alright," he said once the door closed. "The dude Vaughn meeting got the million. Vaughn planning to kill him after the exchange. Warehouse on the south side. Thirty minutes."

"Jacques," I screamed. "He's going to kill Jacques!"

"Everybody strap up," Keisha said. "Let's handle this."

THE WAREHOUSE

"I just got word he ready," Vaughn said, rushing me to the car. "Let's go."

I moved fast.

The .45 went into my purse.
The .380 stayed hidden under my dress.

"If he think he killing Jacques," I thought, "he got another thing coming."

We pulled up.

Jacques stood there, calm. Alive. Beautiful.

I wanted to run to him.

But I stayed still.

"Where my money, bitch boy?" Vaughn sneered.

Jacques lifted the bag.
"Right here."

Engines roared.

Cars surrounded us.

Doors flew open.

Guns raised.

Jonsai.
Devin.
The crew.

Then another voice cut through the chaos.

"Bae—what the fuck is this?" Vaughn snapped. "You set me up?"

A man stepped forward from the shadows.

"Nigga... she not your bae."

My heart stopped.

"That's my daughter."

"HEDRICK?!" Vaughn screamed. "You supposed to be dead! I was at the funeral!"

"What you doing with my child?" my father asked calmly.

Vaughn laughed.
"Fucking her. Same way I fucked your wife."

Jacques raised his gun.

I stepped in front of it.

Then I turned.

And aimed my father's .45 at Vaughn's chest.

"AZALIYAH—NO!" my mother screamed from behind us.

I pulled the trigger.

Vaughn dropped.

My mother ran to him, collapsing, holding his body.

"This is your father," she sobbed. "I was going to tell you when I got back from Atlanta—"

She looked up.

Saw Hedrick.

Screamed.

"I thought you were dead!"

My father took the gun from my hand.

POW.

My chest seized.

Smoke poured into the air.

My vision blurred.

Bodies dropped around me.

I tried to run.

My legs gave out.

The floor rushed up.

And then—

Darkness.

———————

AFTERMATH — THE GOD OF KARMA

Darkness.

Not sleep—absence.

Then—

Drip.
Drip.
Drip.

Cold water hit my cheek.

I gasped awake.

My wrists burned.

Rope.

Tight.

I was tied to a chair.

My head throbbed as I tried to move, but my body answered with pain instead. The room smelled like mold, rust, and something older... like decay that had been breathing for centuries.

An abandoned house.

Walls cracked and peeling. Floorboards warped and stained. One bare bulb swung from the ceiling, flickering like it might give up at any second.

I tried to scream.

My throat worked—but no sound came out.

Then I felt it.

I wasn't alone.

Footsteps echoed slowly across the room.

Measured.

Unrushed.

Whoever—or whatever—was coming knew I couldn't go anywhere.

A figure stepped into the light.

Tall.
Too tall.

Its body looked human at first glance, but nothing about it felt alive. Skin the color of ash and bronze, etched with symbols that moved when I blinked. Eyes black as oil, reflecting not the room—but me.

My breath shook.

"W-who are you?" I whispered.

The air thickened.

When it spoke, the voice didn't come from its mouth.

It came from everywhere.

"I am ROLUNISIS."

The light flickered violently.

"God of Karma.
Keeper of Balance.
Collector of Debts."

My heart slammed against my ribs.

"I—I don't understand," I said. "Where am I?"

ROLUNISIS tilted its head slightly, studying me the way a butcher studies meat.

"You are where all bloodlines eventually arrive."
"Between consequence… and truth."

The room changed.

The walls bled shadows—moving images flashing like broken memories.

My father.
The gun.
Vaughn falling.
My mother screaming.
The smoke.

I squeezed my eyes shut.

"Stop!" I cried. "Please!"

ROLUNISIS stepped closer.

The floor cracked beneath its feet.

"You asked for vengeance."
"You planned it."
"You executed it."

Its eyes burned brighter.

"Did you believe blood could be spilled without payment?"

Tears streamed down my face.

"He killed my father," I sobbed. "He deserved it!"

The god raised one long, clawed finger.

The room went silent.

"DESERVE," it said, slowly,
"is a word humans use to lie to themselves."

The shadows shifted again.

This time, I saw myself.

Lying.
Manipulating.
Using love as a weapon.
Pulling triggers—literal and emotional.

"You took a life," ROLUNISIS continued.
"But you also took innocence.
Trust.
Blood not meant for the altar."

I shook violently against the ropes.

"What do you want from me?" I screamed.

ROLUNISIS leaned down until its face was inches from mine.

Its breath smelled like smoke and rain.

"I do not want," it whispered.
"I collect."

The rope around my wrists tightened on its own.

"Your family has borrowed from Karma for generations."
"Fathers faking death."
"Mothers hiding truth."
"Daughters becoming weapons."

Its eyes locked into mine.

"And now… the debt is yours."

The bulb above us shattered.

Darkness swallowed the room.

I felt something press against my chest—not hands, but judgment.

"You will live," ROLUNISIS said.
"But nothing you love will ever remain untouched."
"Every choice from this moment forward will echo."

I screamed as the ropes finally snapped—

And the floor dropped out beneath me.

CHAPTER 2- Daily Doses

"There is no limit to what we, as women, can accomplish."
—Michelle Obama

"Wake up, Cleo. Wake up, Dannie. Come on—daycare time."

I walked down the narrow hallway, tapping lightly on bedroom doors, already calculating the minutes in my head. Cleo—short for Cleopatra—was my seven-year-old firecracker. Dannie, my six-year-old shadow, followed her lead everywhere. They were impossible to miss: light skin, red curls, freckles scattered like constellations. Cleo had rosy cheeks and bright blue eyes. Dannie had one hazel eye and one green. People always stared. Some called it rare. Others whispered unnatural. I just called it my babies.

"Mommy, I don't wanna go to school," Cleo groaned, burying her face into the pillow. "The food is nasty, and Ms. Phillips stink."

"Yeah," Dannie chimed in, rubbing his eyes. "Her breath smell like boo-boo diapers."

I laughed harder than I should have—because, honestly, they weren't wrong.

"Well," I said, helping them out of bed, "Mommy has to work. And working pays the bills and puts food in those bellies you love so much. So daycare it is. Now go brush your teeth."

After getting dressed, we caught the bus just as the sun started warming the pavement.

"Tell you what," I said, crouching down to their level. "If you do good today, I'll buy both of you a chocolate sundae."

"Deal!" they shouted together, grinning wide.

I walked them into daycare, kissed their foreheads, and headed to work with that familiar knot already tightening in my chest.

The day dragged. Calls back-to-back. Voices blending together. My boss, Adam, paced more than usual—short temper, tight jaw. When I finally glanced at the clock and saw it was time to go, relief washed over me.

I gathered my things and stood up.

"Kyn'Daiyah," Adam snapped, "I need you to stay late."

"I can't," I said carefully. "It's Friday, and because of the holiday the daycare closes at five."

He stepped closer. "Do you want your job?"

I swallowed.

"Sit back down," he yelled, "or daycare won't be the only thing foreclosing today."

So I sat.

I texted my mother. No response. I called. Straight to voicemail.

I worked like a bull watching red—eyes glued to the clock, heart pounding. When it finally hit 5:00 p.m., Adam walked over like nothing had happened.

"You can clock out now."

I didn't respond. I ran.

It took two hours to reach the daycare because of the holiday traffic.

Two hours too late.

As soon as I stepped off the bus, my heart dropped.

Two women were forcing my children into the backseat of a car.

"What are you doing?" I screamed. "I'm here—I'm here now! Please, get my children out of the car!"

I tried to run toward them, but police officers grabbed me, holding me back as Cleo and Dannie kicked and screamed, clawing at the doors, crying out for me.

"Mommy!" Cleo wailed.

My chest felt like it was caving in.

"Ms. Brown," one of the women said calmly, as if this were routine. "My name is Shunda. If you want to see your children again, call the number on this paper and schedule an appointment with Mr. Gabbs."

She pressed the paperwork into my shaking hands and turned back toward the car.

"Wait—please!" I cried. "I had to work late! I'm begging you!"

The car doors slammed.

I tried to chase after them, but the officers forced me to the ground.

"Ma'am, calm down or you will be arrested," one of them shouted.

I collapsed onto my knees and screamed until my throat burned.

"Next time you'll be on time," Ms. Phillips said, standing in the doorway with a slow, satisfied smile.

"You did this?" I yelled. "You bitter old bitch! Why would you do this to me?"

"I was late for church because of you," she snapped. "You were late picking up your kids, and I had to close. Young people need to be taught a lesson."

"I hope you go straight to hell," I screamed. "Nothing you did was an act of God!"

"After you," she shot back, slamming the daycare doors shut.

I went home alone.

That night, I called the number on the paper eight times. I left eight voicemails. No one called back.

The next morning, my phone finally rang.

"Hello?" I answered, my voice barely holding together.

"Good morning, Ms. Brown. This is Mr. Gabbs. You have court scheduled for the 16th at 8:00 a.m. Please bring your ID, proof of employment, and a valid reason for being late when picking up your two children. The address and details have been sent to your phone."

"Please," I whispered. "Can I see my babies until then? The 16th is over two weeks away. They need me."

"No," he replied flatly. "You are not permitted within one hundred feet of the facility. If you violate this order, you will be arrested and charged with child endangerment, along with additional charges related to this case. Goodbye, Ms. Brown."

The line went dead.

I cried every day for two weeks straight.

I blamed Adam for every single moment.

The following week, Adam stopped coming to work. The new manager said he wasn't answering calls or showing up, so he was terminated. That didn't make sense—Adam never missed a day.

When the 16th finally arrived, my hands wouldn't stop shaking.

I arrived at the courthouse at 7:30 a.m. and sat in silence until my name echoed through the room.

"Kyn'Daiyah Brown?"

I stood and walked into the courtroom, my hands trembling.

"Do you have legal representation today?" the judge asked.

"No, sir," I replied. "I brought everything Mr. Gabbs asked me to bring."

He flipped through the paperwork slowly.

"According to these records, you were two hours late picking up your children—Cleopatra Brown and Darren Brown. Is that correct?"

"Yes," I said quickly. "But I had to work late. My mother wasn't answering, and my boss wrote a statement explaining—"

"Ms. Brown," the judge interrupted, "do you own a vehicle?"

"No, sir, but if you would just look—"

"And did your employer know the time you were required to pick up your children?"

"Yes," I said. "But he told me he would fire me if I left my chair."

The judge leaned forward.

"So your job was more important than the well-being of your children?"

My breath caught.

"I never said that—"

"Kyn'Daiyah Brown," he continued, unmoved, "you will not be permitted to see your children until you complete six weeks of parenting classes. You will submit to weekly drug testing and return to this court on September 26th at 8:00 a.m."

The room began to spin.

"I never said my job was more important," I cried. "Six weeks? September 26th is three months away. Please—I need to see my children."

The judge ordered me removed from the courtroom.

A stack of paperwork was shoved into my hands as I was escorted out.

I did everything they asked.

Every class. Every test. Every week.

I marked off each day on my calendar like it was a lifeline.

On day thirty, I woke up, got dressed for work, and reached for my calendar when my phone rang.

"Hello?" I answered.

"Is this Kyn'Daiyah Brown?" a woman asked.

"Yes. Who is this?"

"I'm calling from Child Protective Services," she said. "There has been an explosion at the facility where your children were being housed. Your children did not make it out."

My phone slipped from my hand.

"No," I screamed. "No—God, please. Not my babies."

I ran out the door and didn't stop until I reached the building.

Police. Firefighters. Smoke everywhere.

I tried to push past them, but hands pulled me back as flames consumed what was left.

I buried my children the following week.

They never let me see their bodies.

They told me my babies had been completely disintegrated.

Three months later, I am still in pieces.

I lost my job.
I lost my mind.
I lost my faith in God.

I was completely gone.

I knocked on Don's door.

"What you need?" he asked, cracking it open.

"Something to take the pain away."

He stepped aside. "Come in. We got hydros, alprazolam, Adderall—"

"I don't want pills," I snapped. "They never help."

Don studied me for a moment, then walked to the cabinet.

"Alright. I got Purple Kush for the body. Granddaddy for the upper pain." He grabbed another jar. "This one's my favorite—White Owl Russian. Helps with the mental pain."

He glanced over his shoulder. "Then there's crack, meth, a little PCP over there. So tell me, ma… what you need?"

"I'll take an eighth of everything you just named."

He froze. "All of it?"

"Yes."

I took the bag and headed for the door.

Don stopped me. "I know I'm probably the last person who should be saying this, but whatever you're going through—God will see you through it. Something remarkable will come from this."

"God took my only hope," I said flatly. "He's nobody to me."

That night, I smoked everything.

I prayed I wouldn't wake up.

But God wouldn't let me die.

I battled drugs for an entire year.

One day, wandering with nowhere to go, I saw people entering a building. A paper was taped to the door.

FREE FOOD AND DRINKS INSIDE

I went in to eat.

Instead, I found a circle of chairs. A woman sat in the middle.

"Hi, I'm Shelby," she said gently. "This is a Substance Abuse class at Faith in Family Services. Would you like to join us?"

"I guess," I said. "I don't have anywhere else to be."

"Sit here," she said, patting the chair beside her. "You'll start by saying your name and admitting you're an addict."

I stood.

"My name is Kyn'Daiyah Brown," I said. "And I'm an addict."

"Why are you an addict?" someone asked.

"Because I had no one and nothing else to turn to."

"You could've turned to God," Shelby said softly.

That did it.

"God turned his back on me!" I screamed. "He let the state take my babies and then murder them! He could've taken my life—but he took my children!"

Shelby helped me sit down, holding my shoulders steady.

"Breathe," she said. "Start from the beginning. What happened? Why were they taken?"

"I worked," I said through tears. "Like everyone else. My kids were clean, well dressed, never mistreated. My boss forced me to stay late or I'd lose my job. I was two hours late picking them up, and their daycare teacher called CPS—because she was bitter."

"Did you explain that?" Shelby asked. "Did you do everything they asked?"

"I did everything," I said. "I even had a statement from my job. I didn't have a lawyer, but I still followed every rule. Thirty days later, they called and told me my children died in a fire."

My voice broke.

"They saved over twenty kids... but not my two."

The room went silent.

"Oh my God," Shelby whispered. "Kyn'Daiyah... we are so sorry."

"The judge wasn't willing to listen at all?" Shelby asked carefully. "You couldn't get any help?"

I broke.

"I'm Black," I said, my voice cracking. "They didn't care. I could've walked in there with the newest car and slammed ten thousand dollars on the table—they still wanted my children. They wanted to take them from me."

My chest tightened.

"So I turned to drugs," I admitted. "I prayed every day that I would overdose and die just so I could see my babies again. I just want to die. It's not right that I'm breathing and they're not!"

Shelby rushed to me. "No—no, no. We are not giving up on you. We are going to get you help, and we are going to find someone who will fight for you."

"It won't work," I sobbed. "God is punishing me. I'm better off dead, Ms. Shelby."

She took my face gently in her hands.

"Baby, the last thing God wants is for you to suffer. If there's breath in your body, it means you're meant to fight. He gives the hardest battles to the strongest soldiers—and you have a calling. You just have to answer it."

Something in her voice broke through me.

I stayed.

I went to meetings.
I ate right.
I went to church.
I started rebuilding myself piece by piece.

Two months later, Shelby rushed in with a smile I hadn't seen before.

"I found a lawyer," she said. "And he's willing to take your case—free of charge."

My heart leapt. My babies had been heavy on my spirit lately. It didn't even feel like they were gone. I could feel them with me.

"He'll be here in fifteen minutes," Shelby said.

I got dressed quickly. My hands were shaking.

"Has he ever handled a case like mine?" I asked.

"He's won big cases just like this," she assured me.

As we walked toward the front of the building, I saw a tall, well-built man standing with his back to us, talking on the phone.

Shelby smiled. "This is the young lady I was telling you about."

The man turned around.

My heart stopped.

"Kevin?" I whispered.

"Kyn'Daiyah?" he said, eyes wide. "Oh my God—am I being pranked right now?"

"Wait," Shelby said, confused. "You two know each other?"

"Yes," Kevin laughed softly. "Middle school. High school."

"We were best friends," I said, stunned.

We sat in silence for a moment, just staring—trying to process the coincidence.

"Okay," Shelby said finally. "Let's use the conference room to discuss the case."

Inside, I told Kevin everything—every detail, every document, every name.

"Do you have the paperwork they gave you?" he asked. "Anything could help."

I handed it over.

He flipped through the pages slowly.

Then he stopped.

His expression changed.

"That's... strange," he said.

My stomach dropped. "What?"

Kevin looked up at me, his voice low.

"Judge Marble Wayne died five years ago—in a house fire. And Shunda Wright is not, and has never been, a caseworker for Child Protective Services."

The room went silent.

"In fact," Kevin said slowly, "she's an escort who retired around the same time Judge Wayne died."

He leaned back, deep in thought, then looked at me again.

"Are you absolutely sure this is the woman who was in Courtroom Four on June eighteenth?"

"Yes," I said without hesitation. "I'm positive. This is all the paperwork they gave me."

Kevin exhaled. "Kyn'Daiyah… you don't just have a case. You have a lawsuit. And beyond that—something isn't right."

My chest tightened. "Please help me," I said quietly. "I have to get justice for my babies."

He nodded and tore a piece of paper from his notebook. "Write my number down. We're going to figure this out."

From that moment on, Kevin worked relentlessly—late nights, early mornings, stacks of documents spread across tables. About a week later, he asked me out.

I hesitated.

I hadn't been with anyone in so long. I was still rebuilding myself. Still healing. Still broken in places I didn't know how to explain.

Shelby noticed my doubt immediately.

"You're overthinking," she said. "Go. You deserve something good."

She bought me a dress. She did my hair. And somehow, I found myself standing at the door, nervous but needing—desperately—to feel human again.

Kevin picked me up and took me to a beautiful restaurant. He opened every door, pulled out my chair, made sure I was comfortable before sitting down himself.

"You look beautiful tonight," he said, then laughed nervously. "No—wait. You look beautiful all the time. Tonight you're just... shining brighter. Wow. That sounded stupid."

"I'm a recovering drug addict," I blurted.

He blinked. "Okay," he said gently. "I figured that from the center you're staying at. That doesn't change how I feel. We've all been through something. I'm just glad you're here—with me."

He reached across the table and took my hand.

I couldn't find words.

After dinner, he took me home. Then we started texting. Talking. Going on dates. Working on my case together. It all felt unreal—like something borrowed from another life.

We visited the daycare and interviewed the staff. No one had anything useful to offer. Ms. Phillips, they said, had quit a week after the incident.

That night, I stayed over at Kevin's house. We ate dinner and went to bed early, exhausted.

At 3:00 a.m., his phone rang.

"Hello?" Kevin answered groggily.

"Is this Kevin Wylar?" a woman asked.

"Yes," he said, sitting up. "Who is this?"

The line went quiet.

"I'd rather not say my name, but I have information about Kyn'Daiyah Brown's case," the woman whispered.

Kevin motioned for me to turn on the light. I grabbed his notebook and pen, my hands already shaking.

"Okay," Kevin said, urgency in his voice. "Tell me what you know."

"The case against Kyn'Daiyah was fabricated — all of it. They took her children and sold them to a wealthy family in Ukraine. The couple couldn't have kids. The CPS building where her children were held is part of an underground operation. They profit off removals."

Kevin leaned forward. "I'm writing. Keep talking."

"They have scouts who photograph children that match client preferences. Then they create false reports to justify removal. The price is fifteen thousand for one child — twenty-eight thousand depending on age. They staged the deaths too. They dug up already-deceased children and placed them in the beds where Kyn'Daiyah's kids were supposed to be. Her children were gone within fifteen days of CPS taking them. Check the bodies again. You'll see."

My stomach dropped.

"After that," the woman continued, "go to 645 Terling Drive. There's paperwork in the mailbox — proof and another address."

The line went dead.

Kevin immediately dialed the Sheriff.

"It's 3:30 in the morning, Wylar. This better be important," the Sheriff growled.

"I need a warrant — now — to exhume my client's children and run forensic testing," Kevin said.

"On what grounds?"

"An anonymous tip that those aren't her children in the graves."

A pause. Then: "You're serious?"

"It was staged," Kevin snapped.

"I'm making the call. Get down there — now."

By the time we reached the cemetery, police lights flooded the grounds. Officers and forensic techs surrounded the graves. The caskets were lifted, opened, examined. Bones were carefully bagged and sent off for testing.

We didn't wait.

Kevin and I drove straight to the address the caller gave us. Inside the mailbox sat a thick white envelope. My hands trembled as I opened it. Inside were files — dozens of them — each containing a child's name, photograph, address, and forged removal paperwork.

A catalog.

A system.

We flipped through page after page until I saw them — my babies.

My breath caught in my throat. They had taken them from me... but they were still alive.

And for the first time since this nightmare began, I praised God through tears.

Kevin carried the evidence straight to the station. The Sheriff reviewed every page, every photograph, every forged signature — and the color drained from his face the same way it had from ours.

Within hours, international calls were made. Warrants were signed. Doors were kicked in across borders.

A police unit in Ukraine located my children alive.

They were home within eighteen hours.

The couple who bought them — along with every official, broker, and falsifier tied to the ring — received life sentences. The courts called it one of the largest trafficking conspiracies ever uncovered. The media called it a miracle case.

My lawyers called it victory.

The jury called it justice.

Two billion dollars in damages was awarded in my favor.

Life moved fast after that. Kevin and I married quietly. Peacefully. Like survivors trying not to wake a sleeping storm. We had a son. Four months later — just two days after I gave birth — we took a small family vacation to breathe again, to exist somewhere that didn't smell like courtrooms and grief.

I remember the restaurant lights being warm. The plates steaming. My children laughing.

Then the room tilted.

My fork slipped from my hand.

A cold wave rolled through my chest like something invisible had walked through me. I stood up — and the world went black.

—

When I opened my eyes, the air was wrong.

Too still. Too thick.

I was sitting upright in a wooden chair. My wrists were bound with something that felt like braided wire and bone. The room was windowless, the walls damp and veined with black streaks like rot spreading under skin. The smell — earth and metal and something sweetly spoiled — filled my lungs.

A girl sat across from me. Young. Pregnant. Crying without sound, tears sliding down her face like she'd forgotten how to sob.

"Aaliyah," she whispered hoarsely, as if finishing a sentence I hadn't heard.

The lights flickered — not from bulbs, but from candles burning with black flames.

Then something moved in the corner.

Too tall to be a man. Too still to be alive.

It stepped forward wearing a shape instead of a body — shadows folding around it like robes. Its face shifted like smoke over a skull, eyes glowing with a deep ember red.

When it spoke, the sound came from everywhere.

"Balance must be paid."

My heart tried to tear itself out of my chest.

I knew that voice.

I had heard it once before — in testimony, in nightmares, in the trembling words of the only survivor who was never believed.

The being raised one long, jointed hand.

"I took Azaliyah when truth was buried."

The air tightened like a fist around my throat.

"I take you now that truth has been exposed."

I tried to scream. Nothing came out.

"I am ROLUNISIS," it said, the name crawling across the walls like living ink.
"God of Karma. Collector of hidden debts. Witness to stolen children and purchased lies."

The pregnant girl sobbed harder.

The candles burned taller.

And I understood with soul-deep terror —

Justice in the courts was never the final judgment.

ROLUNISIS had come to collect his own.

CHAPTER 3- THE COST OF BETRAYAL

"Sometimes the person you'd take a bullet for is the one standing behind the trigger."

"How could you, Daven?" I screamed, pacing back and forth, 9mm clutched in my shaking hands. "I trusted you! I loved you! I let you into my life when no one else was allowed! And you—" I pointed at him—"you said you loved me! You said we could get through anything!"

"Ty… just calm down… please, we can talk this out," Ka'Miyal pleaded, her voice trembling.

I spun on her, fury consuming me. "You're supposed to be my best friend! And here you are… sleeping with my man! And you have the nerve to want to talk it out? Shut up!"

I swung the gun, pistol-whipping her across the cheek.

"NNOOO!! STOP, TY!! I LOVE YOU! THIS ISN'T THE WAY TO FIX THIS—PLEA…" Daven dropped to his knees, his hands raised, his voice cracking.

I couldn't believe it. My best friend and my fiancé… behind my back. All the signs had been there, I just hadn't wanted to see them. And now, so close to our wedding day? It was unthinkable.

I know what you're wondering—how it all went down, right? Well… since we're stuck here with nothing but time, I might as well tell you.

I remember the first day I met Daven. We were juniors in high school, and the school dance was two weeks away. Ka'Miyal had been pressuring me to talk to her cousin's friend, Jay's homeboy, but I kept refusing. I wasn't interested in boys, relationships, drama, or anything that came with a mess at the end of it.

Then, Friday morning, my phone buzzed with a text:

"Girl, my cousin and his homeboy are coming to the skating rink tonight, and you are coming. No excuses. I'm taking my mom's car—pick you up at 8. Love, Miyal :)"

I rolled my eyes but felt a spark of curiosity. Little did I know, that night would be the beginning of everything I thought I knew about love, loyalty, and betrayal... unraveling before my eyes.

I had a long week—testing, pre-college courses, the whole grind—so I was more than ready to get out and breathe. After school, I went home, grabbed a quick bite, got dressed, and caught up on the latest episode of The Dazzling Dolls before heading out.

"Beep! Beep!" Ka'Miyal honked from the street, blowing for me to come outside.

Once we arrived at the skating rink, she immediately launched into her usual chatter about Jay's friend—how he had a football scholarship, how his parents were basically loaded. Honestly, I barely listened. I was there for the roller rink, the carefree music, and maybe a funnel cake or two.

"OMG! There they are, come on!" Ka'Miyal tugged me onto the floor.

"Hey, cousin!" she yelled, hugging Jay tightly.

"What's up, MiMi! And daaamn—HEY TY GIRL!" he said, flashing that perfect smile.

I smiled back, awkward but intrigued.

"This is Daven," Jay said, gesturing toward him. "Daven, this is Ty—the girl I was telling you about."

I couldn't lie—Daven was something else. Standing at least 6'2, lean and strong, chocolate skin glowing under the rink lights, perfect teeth, that smile... straight out of a magazine.

"Hi, Miss Ty. Want to join me on the floor? The sidelines can get boring," he said, sliding his hand gently around my waist to guide me forward.

"Okay," I murmured, a small smile tugging at my lips.

"Don't bring her back!" Ka'Miyal laughed. "Y'all have fun now."

So we skated. And we talked—college, goals, our dislikes, little jokes, and dreams. Everything was flowing, effortless.

But then doubt crept in. Why am I opening up to him? I wondered. He's too nice... he must want something...

Before I knew it, I was skating off the floor, pulling off my skates, slipping into my shoes, and heading toward the exit.

"Ty!!!" Ka'Miyal called after me.

"What did you do?" she asked Daven, frowning.

"Nothing, I swear!" he replied, looking confused. "We were having a good time and then she ran off... I'll go check on her. Stay here."

And with that, he took off toward the doors.

I stood in the parking lot, staring up at the sky, heart racing, trying to convince myself to just catch a taxi home.

"It's beautiful, huh?" Daven said.

I turned, and there he was, standing right behind me.

"Why did you run off? What did I say?" he asked.

"Why are you being so… nice? Asking all these questions like you care?" I shot back, walking away. "Boys don't care about anything but their pride and who they can impress—or who they can hook up with in one night."

He caught my arm gently, turning me toward him. "Come here, Ty. I don't know what kind of boys you've met, but I'm nothing like that."

"I haven't been with anyone," I said, yanking my arm back, a small smile tugging at my lips. "But I know boys… they cause trouble."

"So, you haven't even been in a relationship, and you're already judging me? That's impossible… I think I deserve an apology."

And there it was—his smile again. That damn smile. He knew what he was doing. He had to know he was that fine. But I wasn't falling for it that easily.

"I apologize that you couldn't keep up on the floor tonight," I teased.

"Keep up? I was leaving you behind! Hell, I thought that's why you ran off," he laughed.

Then he stepped closer, lifting my chin with his hand. "You're beautiful and smart. I understand why you shut people out… but sometimes opening up can heal whatever is making you lock yourself away."

And just like that, he kissed my forehead.

After that night, we were inseparable. We talked before school, during school, after his practices. He came to see me, took me out for air, and we shared everything under the sun—even plans for the future. Kids. I know—who would've thought I'd be planning kids with anyone?

Life kept moving. Daven's dad passed away, leaving everything to him. Soon after graduation, Daven proposed, and we moved into one of the houses his father left him. Now, he ran two multi-million-dollar companies, and I was working on my Master's in college.

It felt like perfection. My best friend had been there the whole time, supporting us. Daven even got her a job at one of his companies. We were living the dream—a real-life fairy tale.

Or at least… that's what I thought.

For the past couple of weeks, Daven and Ka'Miyal had been staying late at work, preparing for some big meeting in a few weeks. I'd been lingering in later classes just to avoid being alone in that huge house. But today… today I couldn't stay. My head was spinning, my stomach churned, and a wave of nausea hit me so hard I could barely stand.

I called my mom, explaining what was happening. Without hesitation, she insisted I come over and take a pregnancy test. Normally, I'd argue—deny everything—but I didn't have the energy to debate today. I grabbed my keys and rushed over.

We sat on the couch in tense silence, the test sitting on the coffee table between us. My mom's hands trembled as she glanced down.

"Oh my God, Ty!! Baby… you're pregnant!" she shouted.

I froze. Pregnant? How?

"We… we've both been so busy," I whispered, fumbling for my phone. "I mean… we haven't had sex since…" I opened my period tracking app.

"I'll be damned," I murmured, staring at the screen. "I haven't had a period in three months."

I passed my phone to my mom. Her eyes widened even further. "Ty, you need to make a doctor's appointment immediately. And you have to call Daven!" she yelled, fumbling for her phone to tell my dad.

I couldn't process it. A baby… inside me… right now? I got up, my stomach fluttering with disbelief and excitement all at once, and rushed home.

Pulling into the driveway, I froze. Daven and Ka'Miyal were already there…

And all I could think in that moment was… my mom just couldn't wait to tell anyone.

When I walked into the house, my foot caught on Daven's shoes by the door, and I stumbled forward.

I looked up — and froze.

A trail of clothes stretched across the floor. His shirt. Her blouse. His belt. Her jeans. Piece by piece leading up the stairs like a confession laid out in fabric.

My heartbeat slammed so hard against my chest it felt visible — like it might break through my skin.

No. They're supposed to be at work.

Then I heard it.

Moaning. Breathless. Rhythmic.
And the unmistakable pounding of our headboard against the wall.

Boom.
Boom.
Boom.

The sound hollowed me out.

My hand moved before my mind did. I grabbed my gun from the hall drawer and climbed the stairs, each step heavier than the last. The closer I got, the louder it became — the laughter, the whispers, the betrayal breathing behind a half-closed door.

I pushed it open.

My world split in two.

Daven and Ka'Miyal — tangled together — in our bed. In our room. In the place where he promised me forever.

Something inside me snapped. I lunged forward, striking him across the back of the head with the gun. He collapsed sideways. I dragged her off the mattress and threw her back toward the corner.

"How could you, Daven?" I demanded, pacing, shaking, the 9mm clutched in my hand. "I trusted you! I loved you! I let you into parts of my life nobody else could touch! You said we could survive anything!"

"Ty — please — calm down," Ka'Miyal begged through tears.

I turned on her. "You were supposed to be my best friend! My sister! And you're sleeping with my fiancé? And you want to talk it out?"

Daven dropped to his knees. "Ty, stop! I love you — this isn't how we fix this — please!"

My ears rang. My vision blurred.

All the signs I ignored came flooding back — the late nights, the secretive texts, the distance in his touch. I saw it now. Every red flag I painted white. And the wedding so close I could taste it.

"Why?" My voice cracked. "Do you not love me? Answer me!"

"Baby, I love you," he said quickly. "She means nothing. It didn't mean anything."

"Sit down," I warned, raising the gun slightly. "Don't test me right now."

Silence swallowed the room.

"How long?" I asked.

They looked at each other.

"Five... maybe six weeks," Daven said quietly.

Six weeks.

My hand trembled as I reached into my pocket and threw the pregnancy test at his feet. It skidded across the floor and stopped against his knee.

His face drained. "Oh God... Ty... baby, I'm sorry — please —"

Ka'Miyal broke down sobbing. "I never meant for this to happen — I swear —"

"Sorry," I said coldly. "That's all I hear. Sorry, sorry, sorry."

My voice hardened into something unrecognizable — even to me.

"Do you think sorry fixes betrayal? Fixes broken trust? Fixes what you just did to my heart?"

I laughed once — empty and sharp.

"Sorry doesn't fix a damn thing."

I forced them down the basement stairs, my vision tunneled and burning. By the time we reached the bottom, they were bound to the two steel poles in the center of the room — wrists secured, ankles fixed, mouths sealed. Their muffled sounds echoed off the concrete walls like trapped ghosts.

I stepped back and stared at them.

I didn't recognize the feeling inside me. It wasn't just anger. It was darker. Heavier. Like something old and buried had finally been given permission to breathe. Betrayal from strangers hurts — but betrayal from your chosen family carves deeper than bone.

I'd never felt this level of rage before. Not even close.

I made the calls next — smooth, steady, professional. Told Daven's companies there was a family emergency. We'd be gone a few weeks. Ka'Miyal too — supporting us through a difficult time. The lie slid out easily. That scared me more than anything.

When I hung up, the silence felt loaded.

They watched me with wide, wet eyes. Waiting. Hoping. Trying to read what was left of me.

Pain like mine couldn't be repaid in bruises. Physical wounds heal. This — what they did — lives in the mind and feeds on memory. The worst suffering isn't in the body.

It's in the knowing.

I left the house and drove without direction, buying things I barely looked at, moving through checkout lines like a shadow wearing my face. Cashiers spoke. I nodded. Smiled. Played normal.

By the time I returned, night had settled over the house like a lid.

I carried everything downstairs and set it on the table slowly, deliberately.

"Ty... please," Daven managed after I pulled the tape from his mouth. "Can we talk? What is all this?"

Ka'Miyal was already crying. "He came on to me first — I tried to stop it — Ty, I swear — I'm sorry—"

Their excuses overlapped. Collided. Fell apart.

I said nothing.

I raised the gun and aimed it at Daven's chest.

"You love me, right?" I asked quietly. "We can get through anything — isn't that what you promised?"

"Yes," he said instantly, voice cracking. "Yes. I love you. I always have. Since the first day we met."

For a split second, my heart reached for that version of him — the skating rink, the smile, the forehead kiss.

Then the image shattered.

Because love doesn't sneak upstairs and lock the door.

My finger tightened on the grip.

And whatever mercy I walked down those stairs with... was gone.

"Lay back," I told him quietly. "Feet toward the pole."

My voice didn't sound like mine anymore — it sounded calm. Too calm.

He obeyed without arguing, terror replacing whatever pride he used to carry. I secured him in place, then dragged the old basement chair forward and tied Ka'Miyal into it. The ropes creaked. She sobbed through the tape, shaking her head over and over like denial could rewind time.

Something inside me felt split — one part watching, one part acting.

I placed the metal bucket down hard enough to echo. The sound alone made Daven flinch. I leaned close enough for him to see my eyes.

"Pain doesn't always start in the body," I said softly. "Sometimes it starts in the mind… and spreads."

His breathing turned ragged behind the gag.

When I switched the torch on, the flame hissed — and both of them jerked in panic. His muffled screams filled the basement, raw and animal, even before anything happened. Fear was already doing the work for me.

I watched his face crumble. The man who once felt untouchable now looked small. Fragile. Human.

And that realization did something strange to me.

I shut the flame off.

Silence crashed down.

I removed the tape from his mouth just enough for words. He gasped like he'd been underwater.

"What made you stop?" he whispered.

I ignored him and turned to Ka'Miyal instead. I peeled the tape from her lips.

"What aren't you telling me?" I asked. "Because this didn't start five weeks ago. My instincts are louder than your lies."

"N-nothing else," she stammered. "It just— it just happened—"

I lifted the gun — not firing, just enough for truth to feel close.

"Wrong answer."

Her composure shattered.

"Okay! Okay!" she cried. "I wanted to tell you years ago — but he threatened me. He said if I ever spoke up, he'd take our son away."

The basement went dead still.

"Our... what?" I said.

Daven closed his eyes.

And in that moment, betrayal evolved into something far more monstrous than cheating.

It wasn't just an affair.

It was a hidden life.

"You... you've been involved with each other for years?" I asked, my voice hollow. "In my house? Behind my back? Who else knows about this?"

"Ty, I was going to tell you when the time was—" Daven started.

"When the time was right?" My laugh broke into something sharp and unstable. "When exactly would betrayal become convenient enough to confess?"

I turned to Ka'Miyal, tears burning my eyes. "You were my best friend. You could have told me."

She shook her head violently. "You don't understand. He's not who you think he is. I was afraid. He said if I ever told you, he would destroy me — and take my son away. He said losing you would make him dangerous."

My thoughts staggered. Nothing felt solid anymore.

Then Daven spoke again — desperate, reckless. "We can fix this. We can make problems disappear. I love you, Ty. Only you."

Both of us stared at him in disbelief.

"Listen to yourself," I whispered. "Do you even hear what you're saying?"

The truth kept spilling out — secrets layered on secrets — hidden meetings, threats, a child kept out of sight, money used like a leash. Every word twisted the man I thought I knew into someone unrecognizable.

"Who are you?" I asked him quietly.

His silence answered louder than anything else could.

He suddenly lunged forward against the restraints, shouting threats, rage pouring out of him now that the lies were broken open. The basement air felt tight — charged — wrong.

I raised the gun with shaking hands.

And then the temperature dropped.

My breath fogged in front of me.

Smoke — thick and gray — began pouring across the basement floor, curling up the poles, swallowing the walls. The lights flickered. The air vibrated with a low, humming tone that seemed to come from inside my skull.

A figure formed behind Daven.

Tall. Draped in shadow. Wearing a mask that looked carved from bone and night. Its presence pressed against reality like weight against thin glass.

No footsteps. No sound.

Just arrival.

Daven tried to scream, but the sound cut off into silence as the figure lifted one long arm. The room seemed to blink — like a skipped frame in time — and he was gone.

Not fallen. Not moved.

Gone.

Ka'Miyal sobbed into the ropes.

The masked entity turned its head toward me.

I could not move. Could not breathe.

When it spoke, the voice came from everywhere at once — layered, ancient, final:

"Witness of betrayal. Bearer of wounded truth. You are summoned."

The name burned across my thoughts like fire:

ROLUNISIS

The God of Karma stepped toward me — and the world tore open.

—

Crying. Pregnant. Bound by fear more than rope.

And I realized with sinking dread —

I had been taken to where the others were kept.

Collected.

Waiting.

Judgment had a gathering place.

And I was now inside it.

CHAPTER 4 – REKON OF ROLUNISIS

The white room dissolved like fog burned off by heat.

Walls stretched, melted, and darkened. The bright silence rotted into a damp, breathing gloom. The air turned heavy — earth, iron, and candle smoke. Chairs scraped softly across concrete as if moved by invisible hands.

When my vision cleared, I wasn't alone.

The room was no longer white.

It was the same dark chamber — the one whispered about in fear and half-memory. Black candles burned with low, blue flames. Symbols were carved into the floor. Chains hung loose along the walls like abandoned promises.

And across from me — sitting in two iron chairs — were the girls.

Kyn'Daiyah.
Azaliyah.

Their faces were pale but alert, eyes carrying the same haunted awareness I now felt inside my bones.

Azaliyah leaned forward first. "You were taken too," she said quietly — not a question. A recognition.

My throat tightened. "I didn't know where I was when I woke up… only that something claimed me."

Kyn'Daiyah studied me. "Rolunisis doesn't take without cause. What broke your balance?"

The question opened the door inside me — and the story came pouring out.

"My best friend. My fiancé. Years of lies. A hidden child. Threats. Control. Betrayal layered on betrayal." My hands trembled as I spoke. "I thought I was the one delivering judgment... but I wasn't. I was just standing at the edge of it."

The candle flames bent sideways — though there was no wind.

"I raised a weapon," I continued. "I was ready to decide who deserved to live with what they'd done. And that's when the air changed. The smoke came. The temperature dropped. He appeared."

Azaliyah nodded slowly. "The Collector."

"Yes," I whispered. "The mask. The shadow. The presence that makes your soul feel weighed." I swallowed. "Daven vanished where he stood. No struggle. No sound. Just... removed."

Kyn'Daiyah's voice lowered. "Rolunisis doesn't always kill. Sometimes removal is worse."

"I heard him speak," I said. "Not with a voice — with certainty. He said I was summoned. That I was a witness of betrayal." I looked between them. "Then I woke up here."

The room answered with a distant metallic groan — like a gate closing somewhere far underground.

Azaliyah exhaled slowly. "He gathers those tied to broken vows, stolen innocence, hidden crimes, and corrupted love. Not victims only — not offenders only — but crossroads people. Turning points."

"Test subjects," Kyn'Daiyah added softly. "Proof that truth always surfaces — one way or another."

My chest tightened. "So what happens to us?"

The candles flared higher.

From the far end of the room, a tall shadow separated itself from the darkness.

A voice — layered, ancient, inhuman — rolled across the chamber:

"Stories are weighed."

"Truth is measured."

"Balance is decided."

Rolunisis had entered the room.

And we were no longer just telling stories.

We were evidence.

A knock echoed — slow, deliberate.

The four walls surrounding the three women cracked at once — then collapsed outward and dissolved into black dust before touching the floor.

They were no longer in a room.

They were in a chamber of shadows — vast, circular, lit by crooked candles and hanging charms made of bone and thread. Symbols pulsed faintly along the ground like something alive beneath the surface. The air smelled burnt and ancient.

A figure stood before them.

A woman in a tattered black habit, fabric frayed to threads. Her posture sagged as if gravity held her tighter than normal flesh. Each breath sounded like it scraped its way out of her chest. Her hands hung low, wrapped in cracked, darkened skin that looked scorched by time itself.

No one spoke.

No one moved.

"This… this is a dream, right?" Kyn'Daiyah whispered. "There's no way that's real."

Ty and Azaliyah said nothing. Fear had taken the space where words should go.

The woman slowly raised one finger and pointed behind them.

"Look," she rasped — her voice like dry leaves dragged across stone.

Ty and Kyn'Daiyah hesitated.

Azaliyah shut her eyes and began praying out loud. "God, I rebuke every—"

The woman snapped her finger toward Azaliyah.

"Your prayers do not travel here, child," she whispered. "He does not hear you in this place."

Azaliyah kept praying — but no sound came out. Her lips moved. Silence answered.

Ty stared in horror. "Why are we here?"

"What did we do?" Kyn'Daiyah asked, voice shaking.

The woman pointed behind them again —

—and dissolved into drifting ash.

Slowly, they turned.

Three tall doors stood where the darkness had been.

Each door bore a name burned into the surface.

TY
KYN'DAIYAH
AZALIYAH

Ty's door showed a terrible truth from her past — not gore, but consequence — betrayal made visible, judgment made permanent.

Kyn'Daiyah's door revealed the shadow of a friend she once trusted — hanging in stillness like a memory that never found peace.

Azaliyah's door held the image of her unborn child's sonogram — but fractured — pulsing with a dark, unnatural glow.

All three women cried out at once — grief, fear, and realization colliding.

Their chairs jerked forward on their own, sliding across the stone until each sat directly before her marked door.

"Who are you?!" Kyn'Daiyah shouted into the void. "Why is she here with us?"

Ty bowed her head, shaking. "God, I'm sorry… I'm sorry…"

Azaliyah wept silently.

Then the air itself spoke.

The voice came from everywhere — above, below, inside their ribs.

"I AM ROLUNISIS."

The candles bent inward as if listening.

"Keeper of Balance. Witness of Hidden Acts. God of Karma."

The doors trembled.

"Enter what stands before you — or be judged where you sit."

With a thunderous crack, the doors swung open. The restraints on their chairs split apart like burned thread.

No one forced them forward.

They rose on their own.

Kyn'Daiyah stepped into hers.
Ty stepped into hers.
Azaliyah stepped into hers.

And the doors slammed shut — one after another — like verdicts.

CHAPTER 5- AZALIYAH'S DOOR — The Truth She Buried

Azaliyah stepped through the doorway and the air changed.

Not hotter.
Not colder.

Heavier.

The smell was dust, metal, and something sealed away too long. The floor hardened beneath her feet — cracked tile replacing wood. Fluorescent lights flickered overhead like dying insects.

A hallway formed.

Lockers. Endless rows.

High school.

Her jaw tightened — but unlike before, she did not look afraid.

She recognized this place.

"This again," she said flatly.

A bell rang — stretched and broken.

A voice moved through the air — ancient and steady:

"This is where you buried your mercy."

Locker doors exploded open down the corridor — BANG — BANG — BANG.

Inside were photographs.

Daven — younger — already dangerous behind the eyes.

Girls beside him — cornered — crying — trying to pull away.

Azaliyah studied them like case files, not tragedies.

"I didn't care about them," she said quietly. "I cared about my target."

"Say his name."

"Vaughn."

The lights dimmed further.

At the end of the hall, a classroom door creaked open.

Room 214.

She walked toward it without hesitation.

Inside were three desks again:

AZALIYAH
DAVEN
ACCESS

On the chalkboard — carved deep:

REVENGE MAKES ALLIES OF MONSTERS

A projector clicked on.

The film rolled.

Not memory — strategy.

Teenage Azaliyah sitting alone — eyes hollow — reading a newspaper clipping about her father's death. The headline blamed Vaughn's company scandal. Lawsuit buried. No charges filed.

Her face hardened that day.

The narrator-voice of Rolunisis spoke:

"Grief froze. Love died. Purpose remained."

The scene shifted.

She approached Daven first — not by accident — but by design.

Laughing at his jokes.
Ignoring his cruelty.
Earning his trust.

Using him as a doorway to Vaughn's inner circle.

Present Azaliyah watched with no tears.

"I chose the wolf on purpose," she said.

The projector flickered again.

Ka'Miyal appeared — younger — nervous — new at school.

Memory-Azaliyah leaned toward Daven and said:

"She likes powerful men. Easy attention. No trouble."

A lie.

A planted suggestion.

A delivered target.

Present Azaliyah closed her eyes — not in regret — but acknowledgment.

"I fed him what he liked so he would feed me what I needed."

"Say it fully," Rolunisis demanded.

"I traded girls for proximity."

The lockers outside began slamming again — faster now — like a heartbeat racing toward impact.

———

The classroom walls peeled away.

Now: Daven's old office breakroom.

Night.

Azaliyah standing in the doorway unseen — watching — not surprised — as another encounter began inside the room with someone she had steered there hours earlier.

She turned away — calm — texting Vaughn's assistant for a meeting slot.

Present Azaliyah spoke to the air:

"I wasn't shocked. I was efficient."

"You measured suffering as currency."

"Yes."

No denial.

No excuse.

———

Roots split the tile floor and rose — black and wet — wrapping her wrists and ankles — not hurting — restraining.

Across from her appeared Ka'Miyal — not chained — but dim — like a candle nearly out.

"You told him I was safe," Ka'Miyal said softly.

Azaliyah answered without softness:

"You were useful."

The room temperature dropped.

Even Rolunisis paused.

Not from surprise — from confirmation.

Another memory formed in smoke:

Ka'Miyal crying to Azaliyah once — asking if Daven could be trusted.

Memory-Azaliyah replied:

"He's dangerous — but predictable. I can manage him."

She never tried.

Because managing him was never the goal.

Using him was.

The smoke shifted again — showing the chain reaction:

Daven's unchecked violence
Ka'Miyal's fear
Ty's betrayal night
The basement
The karmic execution
Rolunisis arriving

Azaliyah watched it like math reaching its conclusion.

"This was always going to happen," she said.

"Not always," Rolunisis replied.
"Only after you chose leverage over life."

The hallway returned — but now every locker held a mirror.

In each reflection Azaliyah looked different:

One crying
One laughing
One empty
One monstrous
One proud
One broken

All true.

All hers.

A final door formed before her:

COLLECTION

The handle was made of scorched bone.

Rolunisis spoke one last time:

"You did not ignore the wolf."

"You fed it."

"Revenge made you colder than the crime."

From behind the walls came the faint sound of girls whispering her name.

Not calling.

Not pleading.

Remembering.

CHAPTER 6- KYN'DAIYAH'S DOOR — The One She Let Happen

Kyn'Daiyah stepped through her doorway — and the world went silent.

Not quiet.

Muted — like sound had been buried alive.

The air felt underwater. Each breath slow. Thick. Delayed.

She stood inside a hospital corridor — lights dimmed to a sickly yellow. Doors lined both sides. Each had no window — only a number scratched into the paint.

Her hands began to tremble.

"No," she whispered. "Not here."

Rolunisis' voice slid through the ceiling like smoke.

"Truth does not rot. It waits."

A gurney rolled past her — pushed by no one.

On it lay a sheet-covered body — small.

Too small.

She didn't look — but she already knew.

"I didn't kill anyone," she said quickly.

The sheet lifted by itself.

Empty.

That was worse.

The hallway bent — stretching longer — until it became her old neighborhood street.

Rain falling. Streetlight flickering.

Teenage Kyn'Daiyah stood across the road — frozen — watching something unfold in memory.

Present Kyn'Daiyah tried to turn away.

She couldn't move.

Across the street:

A girl was being cornered behind a car by two older boys.

Crying. Saying stop. Saying no.

Memory-Kyn'Daiyah stood beside a mailbox — phone in hand — recording.

Not helping.

Not calling anyone.

Recording.

"I was scared," present Kyn'Daiyah said immediately.

The memory version zoomed in — showing her face.

Not scared.

Focused.

Filming.

"Say what you told yourself," Rolunisis commanded.

Her throat tightened.

"...That it wasn't my problem."

The scene rewound slightly.

Audio returned.

Memory-Kyn'Daiyah whispering to her friend beside her:

"Don't get involved — this could go viral."

The word echoed — viral — viral — viral

The rain turned black.

The boys dragged the girl out of frame.

The phone camera kept recording.

Present Kyn'Daiyah collapsed to her knees.

"I deleted it later — I deleted it!"

"After you sent it."

The ground cracked open — revealing message bubbles floating upward like drowned ghosts.

Forwarded
Forwarded
Forwarded
Forwarded

One message circled in red:

"Don't say it came from me."

The setting shifted again.

School office.

Principal's desk.

The victim's mother crying.

Police asking questions.

Memory-Kyn'Daiyah sitting in a chair — shaking her head.

"I didn't see anything clearly."

Lie.

Lie.

Lie.

Each word carved itself into the walls.

"I thought if I told the truth they'd come after me," she whispered now.

"So you came after her instead."

"I didn't touch her!"

"You removed her shield."

The office melted into a bedroom.

Dark.

Fan turning slowly overhead.

The girl from the video sitting alone on the bed — staring forward — hollow.

Phone buzzing nonstop.

Messages cruel. Mocking. Laughing.

The video still spreading — even after Kyn'Daiyah "deleted" it.

The girl looked up — directly at present Kyn'Daiyah.

"You were right there," she said calmly.
"You could have stopped it before it started."

A chair appeared behind Kyn'Daiyah and forced her to sit — same style as the one in Rolunisis' chamber.

Straps tightened.

She couldn't look away.

Calendar pages ripped off the wall rapidly.

Three weeks later.

Ambulance lights.

Front yard full of neighbors.

Whispers.

The girl never returned to school.

Cause never officially released.

But Kyn'Daiyah knew.

"I didn't mean for that to happen," she cried.

"Intent does not erase outcome."

The sky tore open above her.

Rolunisis' silhouette formed in the wound in reality — antlered, crowned, faceless.

"You did not strike."

"You did not plan."

"You did not lure."

"You witnessed."

"And chose advantage over intervention."

The words slammed like doors.

Mirrors rose from the ground around her — each showing a different version of that night:

One where she yelled
One where she called police
One where she crossed the street
One where she scared them off
One where the girl lived

She screamed and shut her eyes.

"I was a kid!"

"And she was alone."

A final object appeared in her hands:

The phone.

Battery at 3%.

Video still playing.

Upload button glowing.

Rolunisis spoke:

"Every evil needs a doer."

"But it also needs a witness who stays silent."

The phone screen cracked — bleeding black light.

The hallway returned.

One last door stood at the end:

COMPLICITY

The handle was cold iron.

From behind it — faint knocking.

Not angry.

Not violent.

Just waiting.

CHAPTER 7- TY'S DOOR — The Fire She Lit and Walked Away From

Ty stepped through her door — and the air turned hot.

Not burning.

Smothering.

Like breath inside a closed car in summer.

The floor beneath her feet was blacktop — cracked and sticky — like melted asphalt refrozen.

A high school parking lot.

Night.

Empty — except for one car with its headlights on.

Her stomach dropped.

"No," she whispered. "Not this."

Rolunisis' voice moved through the heat like distant thunder:

"Revenge is a seed. You planted yours early."

The car radio was playing — distorted — slowed — warped like a dying cassette.

Inside the car sat a teenage boy — shaking — crying — reading messages on his phone.

Ty recognized him instantly.

Marcus Reed.

Quiet. Shy. Too trusting.

She backed away.

"I didn't touch him," she said quickly.

"You touched his world."

Memory unfolded around her.

Lunchroom.

Teen Ty laughing with friends.

Marcus approaching — nervous — holding a note.

A confession letter.

He liked her.

Had liked her for years.

Present Ty closed her eyes.

"I told him no."

"You told him publicly."

The memory sharpened.

She didn't just say no.

She read the letter out loud.

Mocked it.

Her friends recorded it.

Someone posted it.

Caption:

"Delusional boy thinks he had a chance."

The cafeteria laughter returned — echoing — metallic — inhuman.

———

"I was a teenager," Ty said, voice cracking.

"Continue."

The scene shifted.

Hallway lockers.

Marcus being shoved.

Tripped.

Mocked.

Not by her.

But because of her.

She watched — walked past — didn't stop it.

Didn't defend him.

But that wasn't the worst part.

The worst part came next.

Phone screen projection in the air.

Fake messages — created by Ty.

Screenshots edited to make it look like Marcus stalked her.

Threatened her.

Sent them to others.

"I was angry!" she shouted. "He kept texting!"

"He texted twice."

The screen showed it.

Two polite messages.

That was all.

The parking lot memory resumed.

Marcus in the car again.

Reading the fake accusations now spreading.

His reputation collapsing in real time.

College acceptance email notification — revoked due to "behavioral concerns."

His hands trembled.

Ty screamed:

"Stop it — stop showing me this!"

But she could not look away.

Rolunisis spoke softer now — which was worse.

"You wanted him erased."

"You succeeded."

Marcus turned the key.

Engine revved.

Garage door closing.

Carbon monoxide warning light blinking.

Ty fell to her knees.

"No — I didn't know — I didn't know he—"

"You knew what isolation does."

The memory froze.

Marcus turned his head slowly — looking directly at her across time.

Not accusing.

Just tired.

"You said it was just a joke," he said calmly.
"It kept going after you stopped laughing."

The world fractured into mirrors.

Each mirror showed a different outcome:

Ty defending him
Ty deleting the post
Ty telling the truth
Ty apologizing publicly
Marcus alive

She struck the mirrors — they rang like bells.

None broke.

The heat intensified.

The asphalt beneath her feet softened — pulling at her shoes like tar.

Rolunisis appeared behind her — towering — antlered silhouette burning at the edges.

"You learned something that year."

She trembled.

"I learned people are cruel."

"No."

Pause.

"You learned cruelty works."

A table rose from the ground.

On it:

Her old phone.

The edited screenshots.

The upload button.

Still glowing.

Still waiting.

"Confess it."

"I wanted to hurt him."

"Why?"

"Because he embarrassed me by caring."

The heat stopped.

Silence.

Truth accepted.

Chains loosened from her wrists — but did not fall.

Partial release.

Not forgiveness.

Rolunisis spoke one final line:

"The world met your rage long before Daven did."

The parking lot dissolved.

Ty's chair reformed beneath her — back in the dark chamber.

Across from her sat Azaliyah.

Beside her — Kyn'Daiyah.

All three breathing hard.

All three changed.

And somewhere in the darkness —

Rolunisis smiled.

The doors slammed shut behind them at the same time.

The sound didn't echo — it buried itself into the walls like a coffin lid.

Ty, Kyn'Daiyah, and Azaliyah sat restrained once more in the black chamber — breath ragged, eyes wide, souls scraped raw from what they had just been forced to witness.

No one spoke at first.

The air itself felt like it was listening.

Then Azaliyah started shaking.

Not crying.

Laughing.

Small at first — then cracking — then breaking loose.

Ty turned toward her.
"What is wrong with you?"

Azaliyah lifted her head slowly. Her face was different now — stripped — colder — the softness gone.

"You want truth?" she said hoarsely.
"Fine. Let it finish bleeding."

She looked straight at Ty.

"Ka'Miyal was my best friend."

Ty blinked. "What?"

Azaliyah's jaw tightened.

"She trusted me. Told me everything. Ate at my table. Prayed in my house. Called my father 'sir.'"

Her voice hardened like ice forming.

"But I needed access."

"Access to what?" Kyn'Daiyah whispered.

Azaliyah answered without looking away from Ty:

"Daven."

The room temperature seemed to drop.

Ty frowned. "Why would you need access to Daven?"

Azaliyah smiled — but there was no warmth in it.

"Because Daven could get me close to Vaughn."

Ty's chair restraints creaked as she pulled against them.

"…What name did you just say?"

"Vaughn," Azaliyah repeated calmly.
"Vaughn Mercer."

Ty's face drained of color.

"No," she breathed. "No — Daven said Vaughn was dead."

Rolunisis' voice rolled softly through the dark:

"He says many things."

"I placed her where he would see her."

"WHY?!" Ty screamed.

"Because monsters open doors when they think you're useful."

The chamber walls filled with more memory fragments:

Azaliyah forwarding Ka'Miyal's schedule
Azaliyah telling Daven her financial struggles
Azaliyah suggesting private meetings
Azaliyah deleting warning messages she never let Ka'Miyal see

Ty began sobbing — not loud — but broken.

"You could have warned her."

"I needed him comfortable," Azaliyah said coldly.
"Comfortable predators get sloppy."

Kyn'Daiyah stared at her in horror.

"She was collateral to you."

Azaliyah finally looked at her.

"She was a door."

Ty's voice dropped to a whisper:

"All these years… you knew what he was."

"Yes."

"And you stayed around us."

"Yes."

"And you let me marry him."

Azaliyah held her gaze.

"I needed to get to Vaughn."

The darkness peeled back — revealing a final image:

A much younger Daven standing beside a man in shadow — Vaughn — shaking hands over a folder labeled:

PRIVATE PLACEMENTS

Kyn'Daiyah covered her mouth.

Ty stopped breathing for a moment.

"That's... that's the same wording from my children's false removal papers..."

Rolunisis spoke:

"Threads are not separate."
"They are woven."

Ty turned back to Azaliyah — eyes burning now.

"You destroyed your best friend for revenge."

Azaliyah answered without hesitation:

"Yes."

"Did you ever regret it?"

A long pause.

Then:

"Every day."

The lights went out.

Something massive moved in the dark behind them.

Rolunisis stepped forward — towering — antlered silhouette unfolding like a nightmare given posture.

"Truth is now complete."

"Judgment can begin."

PICK YOUR POISON

ROLUNISIS: THE AFTERTASTE

CHAPTER ONE- *The Cup Does Not Tremble*

The chains did not break.

They *released*.

Metal loosened its grip from Ty's wrists first—slow, deliberate—like something deciding she was no longer worth holding. She collapsed forward, breath ripping from her chest as feeling rushed back into her arms. Across the chamber, Kyn'Daiyah gasped when the iron around her ankles slid open and dissolved into dust.

Neither screamed.

They were too afraid of what might change its mind.

Azaliyah remained bound.

She noticed immediately.

Her chains tightened—not painfully, but possessively. As if the chamber itself had made a choice.

Rolunisis stepped forward, his form carved from shadow and judgment, his voice neither loud nor cruel.

"You are dismissed," he said to Ty and Kyn'Daiyah.

Ty staggered upright. "What about her?"

Rolunisis did not look at Azaliyah when he answered.

"She is not a prisoner."

Kyn'Daiyah's voice broke. "Then what is she?"

Rolunisis turned his head just enough for them to see the truth in his eyes.

"She is deciding."

The floor beneath Ty and Kyn'Daiyah opened—not violently, but mercifully—light swallowing them whole before either could speak Azaliyah's name again.

Silence sealed behind them.

Azaliyah exhaled.

Not relief.

Recognition.

"So," she said quietly, lifting her chin. "You let them go."

Rolunisis circled her slowly.

"I let *you* stay."

She laughed—short, bitter. "You think that makes you different from me?"

That stopped him.

Good.

"You placed her where he would see her," Rolunisis said. "You erased warnings. You fed trust to predators and called it strategy."

Azaliyah's eyes darkened. "I did what I had to do."

Rolunisis stepped closer. The chamber responded—walls tightening, shadows leaning in.

"So did I," he said.

A cup appeared between them.

Not floating.
Not glowing.

Simple. Heavy. Final.

Inside it—something darker than liquid. Thicker than blood.

Azaliyah stared at it.

"What happens if I don't drink?"

Rolunisis didn't answer right away.

Then, softly:
"You will keep pretending you are nothing like me."

That landed.

Her jaw tightened. "And if I do?"

Rolunisis met her eyes fully now.

"Then betrayal will never hide from you again."

She looked at the cup.

She saw every moment she chose silence over loyalty.
Strategy over mercy.
Access over people.

She saw herself reflected—not broken.

Aligned.

"You don't punish betrayal," she said slowly. "You punish consequence."

"Yes."

Azaliyah wrapped her fingers around the cup.

For the first time, her hand *shook*.

"Say it," she demanded.

Rolunisis' voice lowered.

"You are already what I became."

She drank.

The chamber screamed.

Not in pain—
in recognition.

Her body arched as weight slammed into her spine—centuries of broken vows, silent witnesses, knives hidden behind kisses. Scales formed beneath her skin—not armor, not flesh—judgment.

Her scream didn't beg.

It declared.

When the light settled, Azaliyah stood unbound.

Her eyes were no longer human.

Rolunisis stepped back.

Not in fear.

In acknowledgment.

"The Widow of Scale," he said.

She looked at her hands—then smiled, slow and lethal.

"I punish betrayal," she replied. "Not sin. Not weakness."

She turned toward the darkness where the world waited.

"And I never forget."

Rolunisis watched her go.

The cup cracked in his hand.

Somewhere—far beyond time—a child stirred.

One who would not judge the past.

Only what comes next.

Book 2 will show just how far one is willing to go. Azaliyah picked her poison... my question to you is ...have you decided to pick yours?

Made in the USA
Coppell, TX
02 March 2026

72695738R00066